THE LOST PATH TO HOME

BONU VAMSI

Made with ♥ on the Notion Press Platform
www.notionpress.com

"I dedicate this book to my parents, my dearest loved one, well-wishers, and all the supporters who have encouraged me and my work."

- Bonu Vamsi.

Contents

Foreword *vii*

Preface *ix*

Prologue *xi*

1. The Unseen Life 1
2. Seeds Of Change 6
3. The Weight Of Trust 12
4. The Weight Of Sacrifice 17
5. The Unseen Sacrifice 22
6. A Fork In The Road 27
7. The Final Choice 31
8. The Loneliness In Success 36
9. A Practical Life 40
10. The Forgotten Island 45
11. The Plan To "Enlighten" 50
12. A World Of Strangeness 54
13. The Price Of Progress 60
14. A Different Kind Of Wisdom 65
15. The Fall 70
16. The Return To Simplicity 74
17. The Circle Completed 78

Thank You 83

Why Aryan & Rishi ? 85

My Journey with the Banking on Love Series 87

Foreword

The author of love tales has finally come out of them, to give us this wonderful story on how a person rediscovers what life is merely. His perseverance on dedicating time for narration is in docile. The title is really apt as Aryan finds his way purpose of life among the circumstances happening around .

- Tara (Sparkling Star)

Preface

The Lost Path to Home is a story born from reflections on life's true meaning beyond ambition and success. In today's world, where we often chase achievements at the expense of connection, this tale explores what happens when we lose sight of humanity and the simple joys around us. Through Aryan and Rishi's journey—from ambition to self-discovery and peace—I hope to remind readers of the importance of friendship, kindness, and finding purpose in life's quieter moments. Writing this book has been a deeply personal journey, and I invite you to join me in discovering what truly matters.*

Prologue

The title "The Lost Path to Home" symbolizes Aryan's journey away from and back to his true self. In his pursuit of ambition, he strays far from the core values of love, friendship, and kindness that once defined him. "Home" here represents more than a physical place—it's the inner peace, connection, and simplicity he loses sight of while chasing success. The word "Lost" emphasizes how he becomes disconnected from these values, while "Path" suggests a journey that ultimately leads him back to what truly matters. The title captures the essence of rediscovering life's genuine purpose.

CHAPTER ONE

The Unseen Life

It was an early morning in the small town of Amaravati, and the streets were just starting to come to life. A light breeze carried the scent of blooming jasmine from the small gardens lining the dusty roads. Inside one of the well-kept, modest houses, Aryan was deeply engrossed in his work. He was a young research student, famous in his town and even beyond for his intelligence and sharp mind. Awards and certificates adorned his walls, tokens of his brilliance in the field of science.

Aryan was the pride of his family. His father, Mr. Prakash, was a strict, no-nonsense man who believed in hard work and discipline. Aryan's mother, Mrs. Meera, was a soft-spoken woman, always bustling around the house, cooking or tending to the plants in their small garden. His younger sister, Naina, looked up to Aryan with a mixture of admiration and awe, often calling him a genius whenever he explained something about his research.

Aryan's room reflected his personality well. The walls were lined with bookshelves filled with academic texts, notebooks, and several neatly arranged medals and trophies. There was a single bed, a sturdy wooden desk with his laptop, and piles of research papers he was working on. Unlike other students his age, Aryan was less interested in fun or outings. Instead, he was consumed by his studies and his future goals, focusing entirely on achieving success and making a name for himself.

Though Aryan was admired by many, he had a unique friendship with a young man named Rishi. Unlike Aryan, Rishi was a simple guy with an unassuming personality. He was not wealthy, nor was he known for any particular academic brilliance. But Rishi had a pure heart and a deep love for nature and people. He spent most of his time helping others in the neighborhood, whether it was carrying groceries for elderly women or planting saplings in the empty plots around town.

One bright Saturday, Aryan and Rishi were walking down the main street, discussing Aryan's latest research project on sustainable energy. Aryan was excitedly explaining the potential of his project to change the way energy was consumed in their town, his mind racing with equations and possibilities. Rishi, who was not as scientifically inclined, listened patiently, occasionally nodding even though he could only understand half of what Aryan was saying.

As they walked, they came across a beggar sitting by the side of the road. The man was dressed in tattered clothes, his hair unkempt, and his hands trembling slightly as he held out a small metal cup, hoping for a few coins.

Rishi immediately felt a pang of sympathy and dug into his pocket, pulling out a ten-rupee note. He crouched down, smiling kindly at the beggar as he placed the note in his hand.

"God bless you, young man," the beggar said gratefully, his face lighting up.

Aryan watched the exchange with a slight frown. To him, giving money to a beggar seemed like a waste, an encouragement to continue begging rather than seeking work. He crossed his arms, clearly unimpressed.

"Rishi," Aryan said after they moved on, "why do you keep doing that? You're just encouraging him to stay like that. If you give him money, he'll never find a real job. You're not helping him."

Rishi looked at Aryan, his gentle expression unwavering. "Sometimes, Aryan, people just need a little help. Maybe he's too old or too weak to work. We don't know his story. And even if we did, giving a bit of kindness never hurts."

Aryan sighed, shaking his head. "You're too soft-hearted, Rishi. Life isn't as simple as giving money and smiles to everyone. You have to think practically. If everyone just gives out handouts, what's the point of hard work? I mean, look at us. We work hard every day to get where we are."

Rishi merely nodded, understanding that Aryan's world was one of logic and practicality. Aryan's parents had taught him the importance of money and achievement from a young age, instilling in him a relentless drive for success. For Aryan, life was about measurable goals, results, and visible success, while for Rishi, life was something more—a mix of small, unseen joys and helping others whenever he could.

As they continued walking, Rishi noticed a group of children trying to pull a heavy cart that was stuck in the mud. He quickly walked over, rolling up his sleeves and pushing the cart from behind with all his strength. The children laughed and cheered as the cart finally moved. Aryan looked on, bemused by Rishi's eagerness to help complete strangers.

"Do you really think that makes a difference?" Aryan asked, raising an eyebrow as Rishi dusted off his hands and joined him again.

Rishi shrugged, smiling. "Maybe it doesn't make a difference to the world, but it makes a difference to them. And that's enough for me."

Aryan fell silent. He admired Rishi's kindness, but he couldn't understand it. To him, the world was full of competition and survival, a place where kindness was often a weakness rather than a strength. He was too focused on his goals, too absorbed in his own dreams of success, to see the smaller, softer aspects of life that Rishi embraced so naturally.

As the sun began to set, they parted ways, each going back to their own lives. Aryan returned to his books and his awards, immersing himself in his research, where everything was logical and made sense. Rishi, on the other hand, went home with a sense of satisfaction, having spread a little kindness throughout his day.

Aryan couldn't help but feel a bit puzzled by Rishi's approach to life. To him, Rishi was wasting time, energy, and even money on things that had no real, tangible rewards. Aryan's focus was on his future, his achievements, and his reputation. Helping others was an afterthought, something that didn't contribute to his goals.

As he sat at his desk, staring at the awards that lined his walls, Aryan couldn't shake the nagging feeling that there was something he was missing—some part of life that Rishi seemed to grasp so easily, yet remained elusive to him. But for now, he brushed it aside, telling himself that life was about success, not sentiment.

With a determined look in his eyes, Aryan returned to his work, unaware that he was closing himself off from the very experiences that gave life its real meaning.

CHAPTER TWO

SEEDS OF CHANGE

Aryan sat with his family at the dinner table, his face glowing with excitement. He had been working on a special project for months, pouring in hours of research and countless calculations. His project was unique—a low-cost, sustainable waste management system for their town. It was a solution he believed could transform Amaravati's growing garbage problem and, more importantly, his reputation as a visionary in sustainable development.

"I've completed my project proposal," Aryan announced, his voice brimming with pride. "If implemented, it can decompose garbage quickly and efficiently. The best part is that it won't require much funding. It's economical, yet effective."

His family looked at him with admiration. His father nodded approvingly, though he was not entirely sure of the technical details. His mother smiled, always proud of her son's achievements, while his sister, Naina, was brimming with curiosity.

"That's incredible, Aryan!" his father said. "Our town really needs a solution like this."

"Yes," Aryan replied, straightening up in his seat. "Tomorrow, I plan to present my project to the municipal commissioner. If I can get their support, we can start implementing it soon."

Rishi, who had come over to Aryan's house for dinner, looked equally enthusiastic. "This is a great initiative, Aryan. Imagine how it will help the town, making the environment cleaner and reducing pollution. I'm glad you're taking it forward."

Aryan nodded, acknowledging Rishi's support. But in his heart, he believed his project's success would be due to his own hard work and intellect alone. He looked at Rishi with a slight air of pride, knowing that not everyone could think at his level.

The following morning, Aryan and Rishi arrived at the municipal office, Aryan clutching his neatly bound project proposal and a small folder containing his awards and certificates. The building was bustling with people, government employees going about their work, and locals lined up to resolve their issues.

Aryan approached the front desk, exuding confidence. He introduced himself to the receptionist, flashing his awards to emphasize his credentials. "I'm Aryan Sharma, a research student and award-winning project designer. I have an important project proposal that I need to discuss with the commissioner," he said, his tone a bit too proud.

The receptionist, unimpressed, glanced up briefly from her desk and replied, "The commissioner is currently busy with scheduled meetings. Please take a seat and wait for your turn."

Aryan frowned, slightly offended by the delay. He wasn't used to waiting, especially not after all his hard work. He and Rishi took seats in the waiting area, Aryan tapping his foot impatiently while Rishi remained calm, his eyes wandering around the busy office.

As they waited, an elderly man, who was a peon in the office, approached the waiting area, scanning the people seated there. His eyes landed on Rishi, and a look of recognition crossed his face. He walked over, a gentle smile spreading on his wrinkled face.

"Rishi, my boy! It's so nice to see you here," the elderly man said warmly.

Rishi's face lit up with surprise and happiness. "Mr. Ramayya! How have you been?" he asked, getting up to greet the man with respect.

Aryan watched the exchange with a bit of curiosity. It wasn't often that Rishi's humble connections came into play. Rishi had once helped Mr. Ramayya fix his leaking roof during the rainy season, working alongside him for an entire day. Mr. Ramayya had never forgotten that gesture and held a special regard for Rishi ever since.

Mr. Ramayya looked over at Aryan, his kind eyes glinting with curiosity. "And who is this young man with you, Rishi?"

Rishi smiled, gesturing towards Aryan. "This is my good friend, Aryan Sharma. He's a research student and has created a wonderful project to help our town manage its waste sustainably."

Aryan, noticing the way Rishi introduced him, decided to emphasize his achievements further. He straightened up, a faint air of pride in his voice as he said, "Yes, I am Aryan. I've won several awards in scientific research, and I believe my project will bring significant change. That's why I'm here to present it to the commissioner."

Mr. Ramayya nodded, though he could sense a slight air of self-importance in Aryan's words. He felt a difference between Aryan's confidence and Rishi's quiet humility. Nonetheless, out of respect for Rishi and his genuine desire to see young people improve the town, he decided to help.

"Come with me, boys," Mr. Ramayya said, motioning for them to follow him. "I'll see if I can get you an appointment with the commissioner right away."

Aryan and Rishi followed Mr. Ramayya down a long corridor. Aryan's initial impatience faded, replaced by a sense of superiority. He looked at Rishi with a hint of pride, feeling that his presence and accomplishments were bound to secure the meeting.

Mr. Ramayya knocked on the commissioner's door, and after a brief pause, they were invited inside. The commissioner, a well-respected man named Mr. Rao, looked up from his desk as they entered. His demeanor was calm and observant, a man who had seen countless projects and proposals come across his desk.

Mr. Ramayya introduced them, mentioning Aryan's project in a way that showed respect for Aryan's intelligence but also for Rishi's kindness. Mr. Rao gave a nod, gesturing for Aryan to take a seat and present his proposal.

Aryan began confidently, detailing every aspect of his waste management project. He explained how his system would reduce the town's garbage problem by speeding up the decomposition process. He highlighted how cost-effective it was and how it could benefit the environment.

As he spoke, Aryan made sure to mention his awards and past achievements, hoping to impress Mr. Rao with his academic background and research experience. His words were precise and well-articulated, each point carefully crafted to make an impact.

After Aryan finished, Mr. Rao leaned back, nodding thoughtfully. “This is indeed a very impressive proposal, Aryan,” he said, his tone respectful. “Sustainable waste management is a critical issue, and your project offers a promising solution. I’ll discuss this further with my team and get back to you soon. Meanwhile, we’ll review the details and see if we can allocate the required funds.”

Aryan’s face lit up with satisfaction. He had presented his work well and felt assured of his project’s approval. He thanked Mr. Rao and gave a confident nod as he stood up, mentally congratulating himself for his hard work and intelligence.

As they left the office, Aryan’s mind was filled with thoughts of the recognition he might soon receive. He felt certain that his efforts and accomplishments alone had earned him the opportunity.

Outside the municipal office, Rishi looked at Aryan and smiled warmly. “I think it went really well. This project will make a big difference, Aryan. I’m proud of you.”

Aryan, still wrapped in his sense of accomplishment, replied, “Of course it did. My hard work paid off. And it shows that with enough dedication and talent, anyone can achieve their goals.”

Rishi smiled gently, not commenting further. He knew Aryan was too focused on his own achievements to see the bigger picture. But he was content knowing that Aryan’s project might bring positive changes to their town, even if Aryan didn’t fully understand the value of kindness and humility.

As they walked away, Rishi glanced back at the municipal building, his heart filled with gratitude towards Mr. Ramayya. Though Aryan’s project was undoubtedly good, it was Mr. Ramayya’s willingness to help that had opened the door. Rishi understood that life wasn't just about personal success but about lifting others and creating moments of connection, however small they may seem.

The project approval would take time, but for Rishi, the day had already been a success. He had seen how a small act of kindness from the past had returned to help them in a moment of need. Aryan, however, was still unable to see the true value of these connections, his world revolving around his individual accomplishments.

With the setting sun casting a warm glow over the town, Rishi hoped that one day, Aryan would come to understand that life's real achievements were often not measured in awards or titles, but in the kindness one shared and the lives one touched along the way.

CHAPTER THREE

THE WEIGHT OF TRUST

It had been two days since Aryan had met with the municipal commissioner, and he felt hopeful about the next steps. He was certain that the impact of his project and his awards would secure the funding he needed. So, when his phone rang with the commissioner's number on the screen, Aryan answered eagerly, expecting good news.

"Hello, Aryan," the commissioner's voice came through the line. "After reviewing your project, I must say it's promising. However, the municipal budget is stretched thin this quarter. We can only offer a small initial grant—enough to get started, but you'll need to secure additional funding elsewhere. Once you make some headway and demonstrate the project's potential, I'm confident we can push for more government support."

Aryan's heart sank. He was silent, unable to fully grasp the idea that the municipal support wasn't going to cover the entire cost. He had thought his project would be funded entirely, but now, he had to face the unexpected challenge of finding additional money on his own.

Without another word, Aryan hung up the call. He couldn't bring himself to say anything, feeling too disappointed and frustrated. For the first time, he doubted if his ambition alone would be enough to carry this project forward.

Determined but shaken, Aryan quickly called Rishi, asking him to come over to his house. Within an hour, Rishi arrived, his usual calm demeanor a stark contrast to Aryan's frustration. They headed up to Aryan's terrace balcony, a place where they often shared their thoughts under the open sky.

As they sat down, Aryan let out a heavy sigh. "Rishi, the commissioner said he can only fund part of the project. I have to find the rest of the money on my own," he explained, his tone tense and disappointed.

Rishi listened quietly, his face thoughtful but not surprised. He placed a comforting hand on Aryan's shoulder. "Don't feel bad, Aryan. I believe in your project. It's good, and if it really can make a difference, there will be people willing to help. You just have to trust in that."

Aryan shook his head, visibly frustrated. "Trust won't get me the money I need, Rishi. I don't need people's encouragement; I need funds to complete this."

Rishi, sensing Aryan's stress, stayed quiet for a moment, letting his friend's words sink in. But his faith in the goodness of others remained strong, and he hoped Aryan would see that trust and patience could yield surprising results.

After a moment, Aryan had an idea. He looked at Rishi, a determined look in his eyes. "Let's go talk to my father," he said. "If I can get him to pledge our house, I'll have enough to get started. Once I complete the project and get the results, I can secure more funds and pay it all back."

Rishi wasn't sure if Aryan's family would agree to this, but he nodded, ready to support his friend. Together, they made their way downstairs to find Aryan's father, who was sitting in the living room reading the newspaper. Aryan's mother was beside him, knitting, while his sister, Naina, was scrolling through her phone.

"Dad, I need to talk to you about something important," Aryan began, his voice serious.

Mr. Prakash looked up, sensing the gravity in Aryan's tone. "What is it, Aryan?"

Aryan explained the commissioner's response and his idea to secure the remaining funds by pledging their house. He tried to present it as practically as possible, emphasizing the potential of his project and how it could bring them not only recognition but possibly even wealth if it succeeded.

"I just need you to trust me, Dad. Once the project is complete, the municipal funds will come through, and we can get the house back without any problem," Aryan insisted, his voice confident.

However, Naina, who had been listening intently, raised an objection. "But Aryan, what if it doesn't work out? How will we get our house back if the project doesn't succeed?"

Aryan looked at her, shocked by her doubt. "Naina, don't you believe in my talent? You know how much work I've put into this. I've won awards, and everyone knows I'm capable of pulling this off."

His father remained quiet, thoughtful, as Aryan's mother shared a worried glance with him. After a moment, Mr. Prakash spoke, his voice calm but firm.

"Aryan, it's not that we don't trust your abilities. We know how capable you are. But you must understand, this house isn't just a building. It's the foundation for your sister's future too."

Aryan's mother nodded, her face showing concern. "We've been planning Naina's marriage, Aryan. There's a proposal from a family in the U.S., and they're interested in her. They have the stability and resources to ensure her future is secure. If we pledge the house, it could put her prospects at risk."

Aryan's shock grew as he processed what his parents were saying. He had always assumed his family would support him unconditionally. He looked at his sister, who looked back at him with a mix of love and worry.

"So, you don't trust me?" he asked, his voice laced with disbelief. "You'd rather put your hopes on a stranger from another country than trust your own son?"

Naina looked down, her expression conflicted. "Aryan, it's not about trust. It's about security... for all of us. I know you're talented, but this is our home. If something goes wrong, it's not just your dream at stake."

Unable to respond, Aryan stood there, the weight of their words settling heavily on him. His mind, which had always been sharp and determined, felt clouded with emotions he couldn't quite understand. Disappointment, frustration, and even a sense of betrayal swirled inside him.

Without saying another word, he turned and stormed out of the house, ignoring Rishi's attempts to calm him. He walked outside and looked up at the evening sky, his mind racing. The stars above seemed distant and unapproachable, just like his dreams now felt.

How could his own family not believe in him enough to take this risk?

For the first time, Aryan felt the sting of reality that he had often dismissed. He had always believed that with his talent and intelligence, he could conquer any obstacle. Yet, here he was, facing a challenge he hadn't anticipated: the lack of trust from those closest to him.

Standing alone under the vast sky, Aryan began to understand that talent alone wasn't always enough. There were forces in life, like family bonds, security, and trust, that sometimes weighed heavier than ambition. The reality of life seemed suddenly much larger, much more complicated, than he had ever allowed himself to consider.

As he stood there, lost in his thoughts, a subtle understanding began to dawn on him—perhaps trust, like Rishi had said, did matter after all. And maybe, just maybe, the journey of achieving his dreams would require more than just his own confidence. It would require the support, understanding, and faith of others, especially those he loved.

For now, however, he could only stand in silence, staring up at the stars, wondering how he could bridge the gap between his dreams and the realities of life.

CHAPTER FOUR

The Weight of Sacrifice

After the tense evening with his family, Aryan felt stuck and restless. He had spent the night trying to think of other ways to fund his project, but nothing seemed feasible. He was still processing his family's reluctance when, early the next morning, Rishi came over.

They met once again on the terrace, where Aryan shared his dilemma in a quieter, more subdued tone. Rishi listened attentively, his calm presence a comforting contrast to Aryan's frustration.

"So, how much do you need to complete the project?" Rishi asked, looking thoughtfully at Aryan.

Aryan sighed. He had calculated everything carefully, knowing each step required precision and specific resources. "I need fifty lakh rupees, Rishi. That's the minimum amount to get everything going," he replied, his voice filled with a mixture of resignation and hope.

Rishi looked at Aryan with a steady gaze, absorbing the weight of his friend's words. "Don't worry, Aryan. I'll try to help," he said reassuringly. "You should take it easy for a while. Stay calm and think clearly."

Before Aryan could respond, Rishi stood up, giving Aryan an encouraging nod. “I have to go, but remember, things will work out. Just trust me.”

With that, Rishi left, leaving Aryan to mull over his words, though he couldn’t imagine how Rishi intended to help with such a large amount. However, there was something in Rishi’s calm assurance that gave Aryan a sense of hope.

Back at his own small, modest home, Rishi lay on his bed, staring at the ceiling. His mind raced as he considered how he could gather such a large sum. He didn’t have much in terms of wealth or assets. But as he closed his eyes, a memory surfaced—an offer made by an old landlord some months ago.

The landlord had been interested in purchasing Rishi’s house and the small plot of land it sat on, located conveniently in the heart of the city. He had offered seventy lakh rupees, knowing the property’s prime location was worth every bit. Rishi, however, had turned down the offer then. The house and land were the last remnants of his late parents, the memories of his childhood tied closely to every corner of the small home. Selling it had been out of the question.

But now, thinking about Aryan’s project and its potential to help the entire town, Rishi felt a sense of purpose. Aryan had a vision, one that could improve the lives of many people. And though the thought of parting with his family’s legacy was painful, Rishi knew he had to support his friend’s dream.

He sat up suddenly, heart pounding with a mixture of resolve and sorrow. Without hesitating further, he picked up his phone and called the landlord, Mr. Sinha, who had shown such keen interest in the property.

"Hello, Mr. Sinha?" Rishi said, his voice steady though his emotions were anything but.

"Yes, Rishi? How are you? What's on your mind?" came the landlord's curious reply, caught off guard by the unexpected call.

"I... I've decided to sell you my house and the land," Rishi said, a small pause giving away his inner struggle. "Are you still interested?"

There was a silence on the line as Mr. Sinha absorbed the news. He had been eager to purchase Rishi's property but had never expected him to reconsider. Thinking quickly, he sensed an opportunity to negotiate. "Yes, of course, I'm interested. But, Rishi, the market has changed a bit. I can't offer seventy lakhs anymore. Sixty lakhs is the most I can give now."

Without a second thought, Rishi agreed. "Sixty is fine, Mr. Sinha," he replied, surprising the landlord with his calm acceptance.

"All right then," Mr. Sinha replied, still slightly shocked. "I'll arrange the initial advance tomorrow, and we can finalize everything in about a week."

The next day, Rishi arrived at Mr. Sinha's office to sign the preliminary agreement and hand over the keys. Mr. Sinha handed him the advance payment with a courteous nod, though he seemed somewhat affected by Rishi's quiet demeanor.

Before Rishi left, Mr. Sinha cleared his throat, breaking the silence. "Rishi, if you don't mind me asking... why did you decide to sell the house all of a sudden? I know how much it means to you."

Rishi hesitated, feeling a deep pang in his heart, but he answered honestly. "It's for a friend. He has a project that could really help our town, and he needs funding to make it happen. I realized it was worth the sacrifice."

Mr. Sinha, who was usually reserved, looked at Rishi with a rare expression of admiration. He paused, thinking of the young man's selflessness and the gravity of what he was willing to give up.

After a moment, Mr. Sinha's face softened. "Rishi, hearing that... well, I can't let you settle for less. Let's finalize the deal at seventy lakhs as we originally discussed. It's only fair, and you deserve the full value for your sacrifice."

Rishi's eyes widened with surprise, but he was too moved to speak. He simply nodded, a wave of gratitude and relief washing over him. "Thank you, Mr. Sinha. I don't know how to thank you enough."

"We'll complete everything in a week, then," Mr. Sinha said, a faint smile on his face as he reached for the paperwork.

Rishi took a deep breath as he signed the preliminary agreement, his mind replaying moments of his childhood spent in the house. He allowed himself one last look at the place he had called home for so many years, memories flooding back. But as he glanced at the papers, he felt a renewed sense of purpose, thinking of Aryan's project and the impact it could have on their town.

He walked out of Mr. Sinha's office with a sense of closure, though he couldn't deny the ache in his heart. He stepped outside, feeling the cool breeze, and took out his phone. With a quick press of a button, he dialed Aryan's number.

When Aryan picked up, Rishi's voice held a note of quiet determination. "Aryan, I've arranged the funds. You'll have what you need to make your project a reality."

Aryan's voice came through the line, filled with a mixture of disbelief and gratitude. But Rishi simply smiled, feeling a quiet satisfaction in knowing that he had done what was needed for his friend and his town.

CHAPTER FIVE

THE UNSEEN SACRIFICE

Aryan waited on the terrace, his heart pounding with a mixture of excitement and gratitude. When Rishi finally appeared, a gentle smile on his face, Aryan noticed that he carried a small envelope. They greeted each other, and Rishi handed the envelope over, filled with the advance payment.

"This should cover the start of your project," Rishi said, nodding reassuringly. "The rest will be ready by the end of the week."

Aryan's face lit up with relief. He reached out and pulled Rishi into a heartfelt hug. "Thank you, Rishi. I don't know how to thank you enough. I have to ask, though... where did you find this money?"

Rishi simply shook his head, brushing off the question with his usual calm. "You needed money to complete the project, so I made it happen. That's all you need to know."

A little surprised by Rishi's reluctance to share more, Aryan simply nodded, deeply moved. "Well, thank you, my friend. You're doing something incredible. I'll start work right away."

They spoke a little more about the project, Aryan's voice filled with plans and ideas, before they finally went their separate ways for the night. Rishi returned to his small home, where he lay in bed, staring at the familiar ceiling.

As he lay there, Rishi felt a heavy pang of sadness. In just a week, he would no longer have this home, the place filled with his parents' memories, the place that had been his refuge. The old, creaky bed, the faded walls with a few family photos, and the small garden he'd tended for years—they all held pieces of his past. He closed his eyes, trying to push the ache away.

In his mind, he imagined his parents' faces, remembered their warmth, their support, and their love. Would they have approved of his decision to sell their house for a friend? He believed they would, knowing how much they had taught him about kindness and selflessness. Still, the reality of leaving the only home he had ever known was a weight he hadn't quite prepared for.

Rishi steeled himself, reminding himself of Aryan's project and the positive change it could bring to the town. He told himself that his sacrifice had meaning, that it was contributing to something good. "This is what matters," he whispered, forcing himself to believe it, even as his heart ached with the thought of goodbye.

A week passed quickly. On the final day, Rishi met with Mr. Sinha, who handed over the remaining amount as promised. The landlord sensed Rishi's quiet sorrow as he packed up his belongings, each item carrying a lifetime of memories.

Mr. Sinha placed a gentle hand on Rishi's shoulder. "Rishi, I know it's hard to let go of a place like this. If you need any help or a place to stay, don't hesitate to ask."

Rishi looked at him, gratitude softening his sad expression. "Thank you, sir. Actually, if you have any spare room, I'd appreciate it for a while, until I figure out my next steps."

The landlord nodded, leading Rishi to a small, unused storeroom behind the main building. It was a humble, modest space with a simple cot, a small table, and a single window that overlooked the bustling street.

"It's not much, but it's yours for as long as you need," Mr. Sinha said kindly.

Rishi smiled, touched by the gesture. "This is more than enough. Thank you."

With his few belongings in tow, Rishi moved into the room, feeling both the loss of his old home and a sense of quiet acceptance. Once he was settled, he took a deep breath, gathered the funds, and went directly to Aryan.

Aryan was thrilled to see him and greeted him warmly, his eyes bright with excitement as he accepted the funds. As Rishi handed over the full amount, Aryan paused, frowning slightly as he counted the money.

"Rishi, this is seventy lakhs. I only needed fifty," Aryan said, surprised.

Rishi waved off his concern, smiling gently. "Take it all. You never know what challenges might come up along the way. This way, you'll have everything you need."

Aryan looked at Rishi with a mixture of awe and confusion. He couldn't quite understand how Rishi could be so selfless, so generous. "I don't know how to repay you, Rishi. No one has ever done something like this for me. Thank you."

Rishi, wanting to keep the moment light, simply shrugged. "You don't have to repay anything right away, Aryan. Just focus on the project and make it something great."

Overwhelmed with gratitude, Aryan hugged Rishi once again. "Let's celebrate tonight! How about a party at your place?"

Rishi's smile faltered for a brief second, though he recovered quickly. "I appreciate it, Aryan, but tonight's not the best time. I have a few things to take care of. Let's meet another day," he replied, his voice soft but steady.

Slightly disappointed but respectful of Rishi's choice, Aryan nodded. "All right, but remember, I'll pay you back every bit of this. You've done something incredible, and I won't forget it."

Rishi simply smiled in response, patting Aryan's shoulder as he prepared to leave.

As Rishi walked back to his new, small room, he felt a sense of peace despite the sadness that lingered. But just as he neared his old home, he stopped in his tracks, heart sinking as he saw the familiar house being demolished, the walls of his childhood coming down brick by brick.

Dust filled the air as the workers continued, each blow of their hammers echoing through Rishi's mind. He stood in silence, watching as everything he had once known crumbled before him. His sacrifice had become tangible, the memories of his home giving way to the reality of his choice.

Rishi took a deep breath, blinking away the sting in his eyes, reminding himself of Aryan's project, of the difference it would make for the town. But even as he walked back to his small, temporary room, the loss of his family's home weighed heavily on his heart.

For Rishi, it was a bittersweet victory, the cost of friendship, the price of a promise he was willing to pay. And though Aryan had no idea of the depth of Rishi's sacrifice, Rishi held onto the hope that one day, Aryan might come to understand the true value of selflessness and the unseen strength it took to let go

CHAPTER SIX

A Fork in the Road

The project was well underway, and Aryan was busy every day, coordinating workers, overseeing equipment, and carefully ensuring everything went according to plan. As the days passed, he could see his vision coming to life, and his excitement grew with every step forward. Rishi visited the site occasionally, offering help when he could, though Aryan was so engrossed in the work that he barely noticed the hours passing by.

One sunny afternoon, Aryan called Rishi, sounding more excited than usual. "Rishi, can you meet me on the terrace? I have something big to share."

Curious and slightly concerned, Rishi made his way to Aryan's place. When he arrived, Aryan's face was practically glowing with enthusiasm.

"What's going on, Aryan?" Rishi asked, feeling a strange anticipation building in his chest.

"A huge opportunity has come up, Rishi," Aryan began, his words spilling out quickly. "A multinational company approached me. They want to buy my project!"

Rishi's brow furrowed in confusion. "What do you mean they want to buy it?"

"They're offering two crore rupees for the project, Rishi! And not only that, they're offering me a permanent research position in their company. I'd be working out of Berlin, Germany. I even asked about you, and they agreed to bring you along if you're interested," Aryan said, his voice filled with excitement and pride.

For a moment, Rishi was silent, processing Aryan's words. But then, a storm of emotions took over him, and he looked at Aryan with a mixture of shock and disappointment. "Aryan, are you seriously considering this?"

Aryan, taken aback by Rishi's reaction, nodded slowly. "Of course I am. It's an incredible opportunity. Think about it, Rishi! Two crore rupees and a chance to work with one of the top companies in the world. We could be set for life."

Rishi clenched his fists, his tone sharp and filled with frustration. "Set for life? Aryan, you're forgetting why you started this project in the first place. This project was meant to help our town, to make life better here, not to be sold to a company that will only care about profits!"

Aryan shook his head, clearly not understanding Rishi's objection. "Why are you getting so upset? It's my project, Rishi. I put in all the hard work and effort. I deserve to decide what to do with it."

Rishi's eyes flashed with anger and disappointment. "This isn't just about you, Aryan. Think about it! If you sell this project to an MNC, they'll use it to make money, selling it back to our country at a high price. The very people we wanted to help will be the ones who suffer. Your project will no longer be affordable or accessible to the people here. You're throwing away its potential impact on our town, on our people."

Aryan crossed his arms, clearly frustrated with Rishi's argument. "Why should that be my problem, Rishi? This is my talent, my project, and my chance to succeed. I don't see why I should give up my future just to keep it here when I can get so much more by selling it."

Rishi shook his head, hurt by Aryan's response. "So this is what it comes down to? Your success over everyone else's well-being? I thought you cared about making a difference, Aryan. But it seems like all you care about is money and recognition."

"Rishi, you don't understand," Aryan said, exasperated. "This is a chance of a lifetime! You may think it's wrong, but for me, this is the best way forward. And I won't let anything stop me from taking it."

Rishi looked at Aryan with sadness in his eyes, realizing that his friend had already made up his mind. He tried one last time, his voice softer but filled with pleading. "Aryan, please think about what you're doing. This isn't just a project; it's something that could genuinely help our town. Don't let greed ruin its purpose."

Aryan sighed, shaking his head. "I appreciate your concern, Rishi, but I know what I'm doing. I'm going to take the offer, and I hope you can understand that."

Seeing there was no changing Aryan's mind, Rishi finally nodded, feeling defeated. He turned to leave, a deep sense of helplessness washing over him. Without another word, he walked away, the disappointment weighing heavily on his heart. That night, he lay awake in his small room, unable to shake the sadness he felt. He had believed in Aryan, had sacrificed everything to support his dream, only to see it sold off to the highest bidder.

The next morning, Rishi awoke early, still feeling a lingering heaviness. Just as he was about to start his day, his phone buzzed with a notification. He glanced at the screen, and his heart skipped a beat as he saw the message: an alert from his bank notifying him of a seventy-lakh rupee credit to his account.

Confused and a bit stunned, he quickly dialled Aryan's number. Aryan picked up on the first ring, sounding calm and matter-of-fact.

"Aryan, what is this? Why did I receive seventy lakhs in my account?" Rishi asked, his voice trembling with confusion and unease.

Aryan's voice was casual, as if it were a simple matter. "I sold the project, Rishi. They paid me, and I returned your money. I didn't want to leave without paying you back, especially after all you've done for me. Thank you for your help. I'll be leaving soon, moving to Germany to start work there."

For a moment, Rishi was speechless, feeling a deep mix of sadness, disappointment, and anger. He had given up his home, his memories, everything for Aryan's project, only to watch his friend choose profit over purpose.

"Goodbye, Aryan," Rishi said quietly, unable to muster any more words. He ended the call, his heart heavy, wondering how things had come to this.

CHAPTER SEVEN

THE FINAL CHOICE

Aryan was bustling around his house, preparing for his move to Germany. He had made all the arrangements and was eager to start his new life, working for the multinational company that had bought his project. As he packed his bags, his parents approached him, their faces full of concern.

"Aryan," his mother began gently, "your sister's wedding is in just two months. Can't you stay until then? It would mean a lot to all of us, especially her."

Aryan barely looked up from his suitcase, his expression hardened. "I've already delayed my plans enough for this family. I want to go to Germany and start my work now. This is my opportunity, and I don't want to waste any more time here."

His father's brows furrowed in disappointment, and his mother's eyes filled with sadness. "Aryan, this is your sister's marriage, a once-in-a-lifetime event. How can you just walk away from us like this?"

"That's your decision, not mine. You decided what was important when you refused to help me with the project.

Now it's my turn to make my own choices," Aryan replied, his tone cold and final.

As Aryan's parents stood there, hurt and unable to change his mind, Rishi entered the room, just in time to hear Aryan's harsh words. He froze, shocked by the bitterness in Aryan's tone, seeing how quickly his friend was willing to cut ties with his family over his own ambitions.

Rishi stepped forward, hoping to reason with him. "Aryan, your family loves you. They're just asking for a little time. Can't you see how important this is to them?"

Aryan turned, his face tight with irritation. "Rishi, stay out of this. This is my family, my business. You don't need to involve yourself in matters that don't concern you."

Rishi fell silent, realizing that Aryan's mind was already set. He had watched Aryan's single-minded pursuit of success slowly turn him into someone distant, someone who saw people around him as obstacles rather than loved ones. Rishi left, feeling a heaviness in his heart, a growing sense of sorrow over the changes he had seen in Aryan.

Weeks passed, and the night before Aryan was set to fly to Germany, he and Rishi were driving back from a late dinner. The streets were quiet, lit only by the streetlights casting shadows across the road. They were lost in silence, each of them thinking of different things when suddenly, they saw a car speed past them and hit an elderly woman crossing the street. The car didn't stop, leaving her lying motionless on the road.

Rishi's instincts kicked in immediately. "Stop the car, Aryan! We need to help her!"

But Aryan's hands gripped the wheel, refusing to pull over. He shook his head, glancing nervously between the woman and the road ahead. "No, Rishi. If we stop, there'll be questions, maybe even a police case. I don't want anything to ruin my plans for Germany. My flight's tomorrow."

Rishi looked at Aryan, his eyes wide with disbelief. "Aryan, she's hurt. We have to do something. This is someone's life!"

Aryan hesitated, shaking his head again. "No, Rishi. My car will be covered in blood, and if this turns into a police matter, it could delay everything. I can't risk it. I'm sorry."

Stunned, Rishi stared at Aryan, unable to believe what he was hearing. Without another word, he opened his door, stormed over to Aryan's side of the car, and, in a moment of raw anger and disbelief, slapped him hard across the face.

"What's wrong with you, Aryan?" Rishi shouted, his voice trembling with emotion. "Since when did you become so selfish? How can you just drive away from a person in need like this?"

Aryan's eyes flared with anger, and without saying another word, he sped off, leaving Rishi standing there alone, his heart pounding in disbelief and sorrow.

Rishi took a deep breath, steeling himself as he walked over to the woman lying on the cold pavement. As he approached her, he realized with a sinking feeling that she was already gone. Her frail body lay still, the life drained from her face. Kneeling beside her, Rishi felt a wave of helplessness wash over him.

He couldn't stop the thoughts racing through his mind, questioning the cruel twists of fate. *What kind of world are we living in?* he wondered, his heart aching. *A poor street vendor, working tirelessly to make a living, meets such a tragic end. And the people who could help... turn away.*

Rishi's mind reeled with anger and sadness. He thought of the driver who had struck her without stopping, the blatant disregard for life, and his own friend, Aryan, who had abandoned her in her final moments. Rishi clenched his fists, feeling an overwhelming sense of guilt, frustration, and disappointment.

Is this the world we live in? he asked himself bitterly. *Where the poor and the innocent suffer while people stand by, refusing to help?* He looked down at the woman, feeling a deep sorrow in his heart, knowing that she had been left to face her end without a single person to hold her hand or comfort her. The harsh reality weighed heavily on him as he realized his own helplessness in preventing her suffering.

Rishi stayed with her for a few moments, his mind clouded with grief, before he eventually rose to his feet, feeling the weight of the night press down on him. The world, it seemed, was filled with people who would forsake kindness for convenience, people who would ignore humanity in the face of ambition.

The following morning, Aryan was at the airport, his bags packed, his heart filled with excitement and anticipation for his new life in Germany. He waited for a few moments, glancing around as if expecting someone, but when Rishi didn't show up, he shrugged it off. He had convinced himself that he didn't need anyone's approval or companionship, that his journey was his alone.

As he boarded his flight, his thoughts barely lingered on the people he was leaving behind. For Aryan, the path ahead was all that mattered. He felt confident, unburdened by attachments or regrets.

Meanwhile, back in town, life continued. Aryan's family prepared for his sister's upcoming wedding, though they too felt the sting of his absence. And though Aryan had left, the silence he left behind was more than just the absence of a friend. Rishi, too, had disappeared, leaving his small room without a word to anyone, his whereabouts unknown.

The people who had known Aryan and Rishi were left with questions, wondering about the fate of two friends whose paths had once been so intertwined but had taken such different turns. Aryan had left for a world of success and recognition, while Rishi had disappeared, his heart heavy with sorrow and disappointment.

CHAPTER EIGHT

The Loneliness in Success

Aryan arrived in Berlin with high expectations. The city was a world away from the warm, close-knit environment of his hometown. He was thrilled by the modernity, the towering glass buildings, and the bustling energy. This was his dream, the place where he would make a name for himself, surrounded by some of the brightest minds in the industry.

But as the days passed, a strange feeling began to settle over him. Though the city was alive with people, Aryan felt a surprising sense of isolation. Berlin was fast-paced, filled with people constantly on the move, each focused on their own lives and ambitions. There was no warmth, no familiar smiles from passersby, no one who stopped to ask how he was doing. Here, he was just one among millions, another face in the crowd, competing in the same relentless race for success.

In his new office, Aryan quickly noticed how different things were. In Amaravati, he had been recognized for his intelligence, his awards, and his achievements. People had known him by name and had admired him. But here, he was just an employee among many, working in a cubicle under fluorescent lights, lost in the crowd of corporate workers. His colleagues were professional but distant, each focused solely on their own work. There were no friendly chats, no warmth in the air. He was expected to perform and produce results, nothing more.

Each day, Aryan sat at his desk, staring at his computer screen, completing the tasks assigned to him without much acknowledgment or interaction. People walked by, but no one took the time to stop or ask how he was adjusting. His manager would pass his desk, only checking to see if he met his deadlines, never stopping to ask about him personally. The recognition he had once been so accustomed to was absent, and in its place was an empty feeling of insignificance.

Aryan found himself wondering about the people around him. It seemed that everyone here wanted to be alone, content in their private worlds. They came to work, completed their tasks, and went home. No one seemed interested in forming bonds or making friends. The silence of the office felt stifling, and Aryan began to feel as though he was disappearing, becoming a mere number in a massive organization, devoid of any human connection.

One day, Aryan met Tina, a colleague from the same department. She was German, sharp-minded, and efficient, with a no-nonsense attitude. She was practical, always focused on her work, and didn't seem particularly interested in small talk. Despite this, Aryan found himself drawn to her, perhaps because she, too, seemed somewhat alone in the fast-paced world around them.

Over time, they began to have brief conversations over lunch or during short breaks. Tina was practical to the core, her view of life straightforward and goal-oriented.

She didn't care about emotions or attachments, seeing relationships as mere conveniences in the corporate world. Aryan found her approach refreshing in some ways, though he couldn't help but feel that something was missing. He noticed how Tina rarely talked about her personal life or her family, focusing only on work, ambition, and practical matters.

They became friends in the limited sense that Berlin allowed—sharing occasional meals and discussing work projects. But even in this budding friendship, Aryan felt a void. There were no deeper conversations, no genuine moments of connection, only a polite companionship that never touched on anything personal. Tina was friendly but distant, and Aryan realized that the people here valued independence over closeness.

One evening, Aryan sat in his small apartment, looking out at the city lights. It was quiet, too quiet. The emptiness of the room, the silence that filled the air, made him feel a longing he hadn't expected. He thought of his family back home, his mother's gentle voice, his father's firm yet caring words, and his sister's laughter. He remembered the warmth of his house, the smell of his mother's cooking, and the sounds of his neighborhood, where people knew each other and cared for one another.

As he thought of home, his mind drifted to Rishi. The memory of their last days together came back to him—the disappointment in Rishi's eyes, the hurt in his voice, and the sacrifice he had made to help Aryan achieve this very dream. The guilt stirred within him, a faint but persistent ache that he could no longer ignore.

Feeling a sudden urge to reconnect, Aryan took out his phone and sent Rishi a message: *"Hey, Rishi. I hope you're doing well. It's been a while. Berlin is great, but I miss home. How are you?"*

He waited, watching the message, but only a single tick appeared next to it. He tried calling Rishi, but the call didn't go through; it was out of coverage. Aryan stared at his phone, a strange emptiness filling him, as if the distance between him and Rishi had grown far beyond mere miles.

The lights of Berlin sparkled outside his window, but in that moment, Aryan felt more alone than ever. Despite all he had achieved, he realized that he had left something precious behind—something that success and money could never replace. And as he sat there in the silence, a feeling of regret began to take root, a quiet reminder of the friendship, family, and warmth he had lost along the way.

CHAPTER NINE

A PRACTICAL LIFE

The days in Berlin stretched into weeks, and then into months. Aryan adapted swiftly to the corporate environment, quickly absorbing the competitive, no-nonsense culture that valued efficiency over everything else. The warmth and values he had once held dear seemed distant, replaced by a growing practicality, sharpened by the influence of his new friend, Tina. Their relationship was one of mutual benefit; they worked together, lived in close circles, and shared an understanding that time was too valuable to waste on sentiment or family matters.

When Aryan heard about his sister's wedding date approaching, he dismissed the idea of traveling back to India. "There's too much to do here, and besides, it's just one day. They'll understand," he told himself. Then, when his father fell ill, Aryan pushed the thought aside, convincing himself that his family could manage, that he was needed more in Berlin than back home. Over time, even his family's messages about their financial challenges felt like distractions from his work.

Tina, a practical person herself, seemed to understand this way of thinking perfectly. She never asked Aryan about his family, nor did she discuss hers. They had both agreed, silently, that family attachments were unnecessary burdens, best left to others who didn't have larger ambitions.

As they worked together on a new research project, Aryan found himself more involved than ever. The project aimed to locate a remote, untouched tribal community—one of the last on Earth—and study their way of life. The idea was to expose them to modern advancements and bring them "into the fold" of modern civilization.

One evening, as Aryan and Tina worked late into the night, Tina leaned back in her chair, smirking. "Imagine this," she said, her tone playful. "We get to their village, and they see us, two people from the outside world, who've come to 'enlighten' them. They'd probably think we're aliens."

Aryan chuckled, though his tone held a hint of sarcasm. "Or they might think we're intruders and chase us out with spears. I'm not sure they'd appreciate us barging in and telling them how to live."

Tina laughed, an unusual softness to her normally cool demeanor. "Maybe. But it's our job to study them, remember? To 'connect' them with our world," she said, making air quotes with her fingers. "Honestly, I think we're probably more alien to them than they are to us."

"Right," Aryan replied, grinning. "We're 'helping' them, even if they didn't ask for it. But I suppose it's all for the sake of knowledge."

Their conversations often held this playful cynicism, a detached amusement about their mission. For Aryan, Tina was the perfect companion—focused, practical, and uninterested in deeper emotions. They spent nearly every waking hour together, working tirelessly, driven by their shared ambition to make this project a success.

Over time, something resembling affection grew between them, though it was practical and calculated rather than heartfelt. They agreed to enter a relationship but treated it more like an extension of their work arrangement—a mutually beneficial decision, convenient and efficient.

One night, over dinner, Tina brought up marriage. "You know, it would make sense if we got married. It'd simplify paperwork and let us present a unified front to sponsors for our project. What do you think?"

Aryan thought about it for a moment and nodded. "You're right. It does make sense. No need for anything big. We can just exchange rings at the church, get the legalities sorted out, and be done with it."

They arranged a small, quiet ceremony, exchanging rings in an empty church with only a few witnesses present. There were no vows, no celebration—just a few formal words exchanged. Aryan took a photo of the ceremony and sent it to his family back in India, with no further explanation.

For Aryan, the marriage was just another step forward, another efficient choice made in the name of practicality. It was convenient, it was logical, and it required no emotions, which suited him perfectly.

As the days went on, Aryan began to reflect on how much his life had changed. He had left behind everything—family, friends, even his own emotions—in the pursuit of success. With Tina by his side, he was living a life that was carefully calculated, devoid of any deep attachment or connection. But was it truly fulfilling?

One evening, as they worked on a proposal for funding, Tina looked up from her laptop and commented, "We're doing well, Aryan. This life—it's productive. Efficient. We're not weighed down by unnecessary attachments."

Aryan nodded, though he felt a strange emptiness in her words. "Yes, it's practical," he replied, though he couldn't shake a quiet thought stirring at the back of his mind—a faint longing for something more than just practicality.

The life he and Tina led was designed for efficiency, but there was no warmth, no joy, and no purpose beyond their own ambitions. Everything they did was transactional, every decision made with cold calculation. In their quest to succeed, to be productive, they had stripped away the very elements that made life rich and meaningful. His marriage to Tina was a symbol of this—an arrangement rather than a partnership, a union without love.

As Aryan sat back, observing his life, he wondered if this was what he had truly wanted. His mind drifted back to his hometown, to the people he had left behind. He thought of his parents, who had wanted nothing more than to see him at his sister's wedding, and of Rishi, the friend who had sacrificed so much for his dream, only to be left behind.

He remembered Rishi's words that night, the last time they had spoken, and the disappointment in his eyes. Aryan had dismissed those words then, but now, he felt their weight. In his pursuit of success, he had become a stranger, disconnected from the warmth and humanity he once knew. He had become practical, yes, but at what cost?

Aryan began to realize that his ambition had made him a part of a larger, soulless machine, where people were valued only for their output, not for who they were. He was just one in a sea of faceless individuals, all chasing after success, all trying to climb the same endless ladder.

As he looked at Tina, who sat across from him, fully engrossed in her work, he felt a pang of sadness. She was his partner, yet there was no real connection between them—just an agreement to live and work together efficiently, nothing more. Their relationship was a product of evolution's cold logic, an arrangement forged by mutual benefit rather than love or compassion.

In his quiet moments, Aryan wondered if humanity had lost its way. In their pursuit of progress, people had become detached, viewing relationships as burdens and emotions as weaknesses. Love, compassion, and empathy—these qualities that once defined human beings—had been replaced by ambition, competition, and self-interest.

As Aryan sat in silence, reflecting on the life he had chosen, he felt an ache that no success or recognition could fill. He had reached his goals, but in doing so, he had lost the essence of what it meant to be human.

He wondered if, in their pursuit of progress, people had turned into something else, something less alive, less connected, and less compassionate. And as he sat there, in the cold, quiet room with Tina working beside him, Aryan felt a sense of loss—a loss that went beyond words, a loss of the very soul that once made life meaningful.

CHAPTER TEN

The Forgotten Island

Aryan and Tina had been working for months on their new project, and finally, they had a lead. They had located a remote, untouched tribal community on an isolated island that had remained hidden from the modern world. It was the perfect discovery—an opportunity to understand an ancient way of life, untainted by technology or modern influence. Both of them were eager to make contact and study these people, documenting their customs, beliefs, and way of life.

After weeks of planning, Aryan and Tina gathered all they needed for the trip, including food, water, some cash, and ornaments they thought could serve as gifts. They hired a local boatman to take them to the island, and by early morning, they set off, watching the mainland disappear into the distance as they sailed into the unknown.

The boat creaked as it cut through the waves, carrying them over the endless blue ocean. Aryan and Tina sat amidst their supplies, their faces lit with anticipation.

"So, what's your bet on how they'll react when they see us?" Aryan asked, grinning as he organized the cash and ornaments into neat piles.

Tina laughed, a bit of excitement showing on her usually composed face. "I'm not sure. They've never seen outsiders, so we might look like strange creatures to them. I'm half-expecting them to stare at us like we're from another world," she said, glancing out at the endless sea.

Aryan chuckled, nodding. "Or maybe they'll think we're gods bringing gifts," he said, patting the box of cash and the food supplies stacked beside them.

The boat rocked gently as they moved further from the shore, the vast ocean stretching out around them. The blue waves sparkled under the sun, and for a while, they sat in silence, simply enjoying the journey. The isolation of the ocean had a calming effect, and for a brief moment, Aryan felt a sense of peace he hadn't felt in a long time.

As they drew closer to the island, a strange tension settled over them. The air felt heavier, as if they were crossing into a different world, a place untouched by time. They could see the silhouette of the island ahead, shrouded in mist, with dense trees and rocky cliffs rising against the sky.

"Look over there," Tina whispered, pointing toward the shore. Aryan squinted, noticing a thin column of smoke rising above the trees. There was a rhythmic, low drumming sound in the distance, carrying over the water.

"Seems like they already know we're coming," Aryan said, his excitement growing.

The boat slowed as they neared the shore. Suddenly, dozens of figures appeared along the beach, their silhouettes dark against the misty background. The tribal people were standing there, watching the boat approach, their expressions unreadable. Some held wooden spears, others had painted faces, and their bodies were adorned with leaves and shells.

As they drew closer, Aryan decided to make a grand entrance. "Let's show them what we've brought," he said, opening one of the boxes filled with cash and holding up a stack of bills, hoping it would impress them.

To his surprise, the tribespeople showed no reaction. They looked at the money with blank expressions, unmoved by what they saw. Aryan tried again, this time holding up some shiny ornaments, thinking the glittering objects might catch their attention. Instead, a few of the tribesmen picked up stones and hurled them toward the boat, shouting in a language Aryan couldn't understand.

"Okay, bad idea," Tina muttered, ducking as a stone sailed over her head.

"Maybe they don't care about money or jewelry," Aryan said, baffled. "Let's try the food and water instead."

He reached for the supplies, holding up packages of dried food and bottles of water. This time, the tribespeople reacted. They began murmuring excitedly among themselves, their faces breaking into smiles. One of them started to dance, and soon, the others joined in, welcoming Aryan and Tina with joyful movements and chants.

Aryan and Tina carefully disembarked from the boat, stepping onto the sandy shore as the tribespeople surrounded them, their faces full of curiosity and warmth. Though they were initially nervous, Aryan and Tina began to relax as they saw the excitement and friendliness in the tribespeople's eyes.

The tribespeople communicated in gestures and signs, as their language was unlike anything Aryan or Tina had ever heard. They seemed to understand that Aryan and Tina had come in peace, and they led them to a series of caves nestled in the cliffs by the shore.

The caves were adorned with intricate carvings, drawings that depicted scenes from their lives—images of hunting, rituals, and strange symbols that seemed to represent their beliefs. Aryan stared at the carvings, fascinated. "Look at this, Tina," he whispered. "These drawings must be hundreds, maybe thousands of years old. They tell the story of their people."

Tina nodded, equally mesmerized by the artwork on the cave walls. "It's incredible. We're seeing a world that has existed here in isolation, completely untouched by modern civilization."

As they explored further, Aryan noticed symbols of circles and spirals, along with images of animals and birds that seemed to hold spiritual significance for the tribe. The tribespeople watched them with quiet pride, occasionally gesturing to explain what certain carvings meant, though Aryan and Tina could only understand so much through signs.

The day passed quickly as they continued exploring, surrounded by the mysterious beauty of the island and the warmth of the tribe. Night fell, and the tribespeople gathered around a large fire, sitting together as they shared food and stories in their language, with Aryan and Tina following along as best they could.

Technology was useless on the island; there was no signal, no electricity, and none of the conveniences Aryan and Tina were accustomed to. Yet, despite the lack of modern comforts, Aryan felt a strange sense of peace in the simplicity of the moment. The fire crackled, casting shadows on the cave walls as the tribe sang songs in their ancient language, their voices rising and falling like waves on the shore.

Aryan lay back, staring up at the stars visible through the cave opening. For the first time in years, he felt a deep sense of connection—not to his ambitions or his work, but to the world around him, a world far older and simpler than the life he had been living.

As he drifted off to sleep, he thought of his hometown, his family, and Rishi. The island was silent, save for the distant sound of waves crashing against the shore. And under the blanket of stars, Aryan felt the faint stirrings of something he had long forgotten—a yearning for meaning beyond success, a desire for a life rich with purpose and connection.

But tonight, he was simply a traveler, resting among strangers who had welcomed him with open arms, unaware of the world beyond their island. And as the fire died down, Aryan's eyes grew heavy, his mind filled with the mysteries of the island, the carvings on the walls, and the faces of people he had left behind.

CHAPTER ELEVEN

The Plan to "Enlighten"

The next morning, Aryan and Tina woke to the sounds of laughter and music echoing through the island. They stepped out of the cave to find the tribespeople gathered along the shore, dancing and singing in a beautiful display of joy and unity as they worshipped the rising sun. Their faces shone with happiness, their movements were graceful, and the energy around them felt pure and untainted by any sense of worry or stress.

Aryan and Tina watched, somewhat amused by the scene before them. To them, it seemed like these people were living in a bubble, blissfully ignorant of the advances that awaited them in the "real" world.

Tina shook her head with a smirk. "It's hard to believe they can live like this, cut off from everything," she whispered to Aryan. "No technology, no comforts—just dancing and worshipping the sun. They're missing out on everything the modern world has to offer."

Aryan nodded, glancing at the tribespeople with a mixture of curiosity and pity. "Exactly. They have no idea what they're missing. The advancements, the comforts, the knowledge we have—it's all beyond their understanding. They're like children, stuck in a time long forgotten."

Tina's eyes sparkled with an idea. "What if we take one of them back with us? A young one, maybe in their early twenties. We could show him what the world outside is really like. Imagine the impact it could have on him, how much he could learn from seeing modern civilization."

Aryan raised an eyebrow, considering her suggestion. "You mean... kidnap one of them? I'm not sure how well that would go over with them."

"It's not kidnapping," Tina replied smoothly. "Think of it as an experiment, a way to broaden their horizons. We'll bring him back, let him experience the modern world, and then maybe return him later with all this new knowledge."

Aryan thought about it, the idea tempting him. Bringing one of the tribespeople back to Berlin would add an entirely new dimension to their project and might even gain them recognition and support from their research community.

"All right," he agreed, a glint of excitement in his eyes. "Let's do it. We'll find someone young and cooperative, and tonight, we'll give him a mild anesthetic to make it easier to take him with us. By the time they notice, we'll be on our way back to Berlin."

The two spent the rest of the day observing the tribespeople, searching for someone who seemed fit for their plan. They soon noticed a young man around twenty years old, who had been particularly curious about Aryan and Tina since their arrival. He had watched them with fascination, his eyes filled with questions, as if he were trying to understand these strange visitors from a world he had never seen.

By nightfall, Aryan and Tina had prepared their plan. They gathered some food supplies and carefully measured a dose of anesthetic to use on the young tribesman, ensuring he would stay asleep through the journey. The tribe had retired to their caves after the evening's celebrations, and the island was quiet, save for the sound of waves lapping against the shore.

Aryan and Tina made their way quietly to the cave where the young man was sleeping, careful not to alert any of the other tribespeople. Aryan held the small vial of anesthetic as they approached the sleeping figure, and with careful precision, he administered it. Within moments, the young man was deeply asleep, his breathing calm and steady.

"Let's move," Tina whispered, grabbing their supplies as Aryan gently lifted the young man and carried him toward the boat. They moved quickly, knowing they had only a few hours before the tribe might notice his absence.

As they sailed away from the island, Aryan glanced back, watching the fading silhouette of the shore. He felt a strange sense of unease, though he quickly pushed it aside, reminding himself of the importance of their mission. They were going to give this young man an opportunity to see a world he had never dreamed of—a gift, he reasoned, even if he couldn't understand it yet.

The journey back to Berlin was uneventful, the young man sleeping soundly under the effects of the anaesthetic. Aryan and Tina kept a close eye on him, relieved that he remained peaceful and undisturbed during the voyage. They spoke in low voices, excitedly discussing how they would introduce him to the modern world, envisioning the ways he would react to everything from cars to skyscrapers, from electricity to technology.

"We'll start small," Tina said, her eyes gleaming with excitement. "We can show him the city, the transportation, maybe even introduce him to some of our colleagues. It'll be like watching a child experience everything for the first time."

Aryan nodded, feeling a thrill at the prospect. "Yes, and imagine the research we could publish. It'll be groundbreaking. People will want to hear about his transformation, about how he adapts to the new world."

Finally, after several hours at sea, they arrived back in Berlin. They had arranged for a private room for their guest, ensuring he would have a quiet and comfortable space to adjust to his new surroundings. As the boat docked, they carefully lifted the still-sleeping tribesman, carrying him into the city.

For Aryan and Tina, this was the beginning of a new chapter in their project, an adventure that promised fame and recognition. But as they stepped onto the Berlin streets, carrying their unwitting guest from an untouched world, they couldn't foresee the challenges that lay ahead—or the impact this experience would have on each of them.

They had brought the young man to a place he had never known, far from his people, his culture, and everything he had ever loved. And as the city lights shone down on them, casting long shadows across the streets, a quiet sense of foreboding settled over Aryan, though he couldn't quite explain why.

For now, though, he pushed those thoughts aside, focusing on the journey ahead and the new discoveries it promised.

CHAPTER TWELVE

A World of Strangeness

The young tribesman awoke in a dimly lit room, his eyes darting around, filled with confusion and fear. He couldn't recognize his surroundings, and everything felt alien and threatening. The walls, so smooth and solid, seemed to close in on him, and strange objects littered the room. He cried out in his language, calling for someone, hoping that one of his people might appear to rescue him from this nightmare. His shouts echoed through the room, as he frantically ran around, pounding his fists on the walls in desperation.

Hearing the noise, Aryan and Tina hurried inside. They were initially taken aback by the sight of the young man in a panic, his wild eyes filled with terror. They approached him slowly, speaking in soothing tones even though he couldn't understand their words. Aryan reached for a bottle of cool mineral water, hoping to calm him down.

He took the bottle and brought it to his lips, but after tasting the water, he spat it out onto the floor, looking at it in disgust. Confused, Aryan exchanged a glance with Tina, who quickly went to the sink and filled a glass with tap water. This time, the young man drank it, his face still showing signs of discomfort but grateful for the familiar taste. He sat down on the floor, exhausted but slightly calmer, his eyes warily following the couple.

Realizing they had to make him look more presentable for the city, Aryan and Tina offered him a set of new clothes. The tribesman looked at the garments suspiciously, touching the fabric as if it were a strange skin. He reluctantly changed, his discomfort evident as he tugged at the tight, unfamiliar fit.

Despite his obvious distress, Aryan and Tina felt optimistic about their mission. They wanted to expose him to the wonders of modern life, and their excitement overshadowed any concern for his discomfort. Once dressed, they led him out of the room, taking him to Aryan's office for an introduction.

The young tribesman's eyes grew wide with fear as they entered the office building, a place filled with shiny surfaces, cold lights, and people bustling around with phones and computers. He cowered, staying close to Aryan and Tina, as unfamiliar sounds and faces surrounded him. Media people had already gathered, eager to hear the couple's announcement about their "groundbreaking" project. Cameras flashed, microphones were thrust forward, and Aryan and Tina proudly explained their intentions, presenting the young man as their "ambassador" to the modern world.

But the young tribesman was terrified, shrinking back with each flash and loud sound, his heart pounding in his chest. He glanced desperately at the doors, longing to escape this overwhelming place.

The days that followed were a whirlwind of introductions to Aryan and Tina's world. Their goal was to show him every facet of modern life, hoping he would eventually appreciate it. However, each new experience seemed to frighten him more, leaving him deeply uncomfortable and longing for home.

Vending Machines

The first stop was a vending machine at the office building. Aryan placed a few coins into the machine, which whirred and clanged as a snack dropped down. He picked it up and offered it to the young man, trying to explain its function through gestures. The tribesman stared at the machine, bewildered, before hesitantly reaching for the snack. But as he brought it to his mouth, he stopped, sniffing it and looking at Aryan with suspicion. Unable to understand why anyone would eat something that came from a metal box, he simply handed it back, shaking his head.

Grocery Stores

Next, they led him into a bustling grocery store, where rows of colorful packages lined the shelves, each aisle filled with countless choices. The young man's eyes darted around nervously, overwhelmed by the endless displays of food he couldn't recognize. He clung to Aryan and Tina, afraid of getting lost in the maze of aisles and strange people. Shoppers glanced at him curiously, his discomfort and unfamiliar clothing attracting unwanted attention. Aryan encouraged him to pick up a fruit or a snack, but he refused, too intimidated by the foreign environment.

Food Outlets

At a fast-food outlet, Aryan and Tina bought him a burger, hoping it would impress him. They demonstrated how to eat it, smiling as they took bites, but the tribesman held it at arm's length, unsure of what to do. The smell, the packaging, the unfamiliar texture—all of it was too strange.

He set it down, refusing to touch it again, his discomfort growing as they urged him to try. The loud chatter, the clinking of trays, and the strange, unfamiliar food only heightened his unease, and he looked at Aryan and Tina with a silent plea to leave.

Casino

They decided to show him a casino next, hoping the bright lights and excitement would intrigue him. As they entered, the flashing lights, loud music, and ringing slot machines seemed to overwhelm him completely. He backed away, covering his ears against the noise, his eyes darting around in panic as people cheered and laughed, oblivious to his distress. To him, the casino was chaotic, filled with bizarre sounds and people acting in ways he couldn't comprehend. Aryan and Tina were oblivious to his discomfort, caught up in their excitement over the experience they were "gifting" him.

Amusement Park

Their next stop was an amusement park, a place filled with dizzying rides and excited crowds. They led him to a Ferris wheel, thinking he might enjoy the view from above. As the ride began to move, the young tribesman gripped the bar, his knuckles turning white as he held on for dear life. He closed his eyes, his heart racing, feeling trapped and vulnerable in the swaying metal carriage. Aryan and Tina laughed, oblivious to his fear, assuming he was simply thrilled by the experience. But to the tribesman, the height and movement were terrifying, a feeling of being suspended far from solid ground.

City Buses, Trams, & Flights

They took him on city buses and trams, explaining the concept of transportation, but he only grew more agitated with each new vehicle. The constant jostling, the crowded spaces, and the loud hum of engines made him restless, and he refused to sit, standing with a tense, fearful posture as they moved from place to place. Finally, they arranged a short flight, believing the view from the plane would amaze him. But the rumbling of the engine, the confined space, and the sensation of leaving the ground left him terrified. He clung to his seat, eyes wide with fear, praying in his own language to make it safely back to the ground.

Days of Discomfort

Each experience only deepened his discomfort, as Aryan and Tina seemed blind to the distress they were causing. With every new location, the young tribesman withdrew further, refusing to drink or eat, his spirit visibly waning. The world they had wanted to show him felt like a strange prison, one that filled him with dread and confusion.

After two or three exhausting days of constant exposure to the unfamiliar, he fell asleep one night, his mind and body drained. In the quiet of his room, he finally found a moment of peace, a temporary escape from the nightmare he was living.

Outside the room, Aryan and Tina sat together, a sense of pride and accomplishment in their voices.

"Can you believe it?" Aryan said, smiling. "We've achieved something incredible. We brought someone from an untouched world and showed him the wonders of modern civilization. This is groundbreaking."

Tina nodded, her eyes gleaming with satisfaction. "People will remember this project, Aryan. We're making history. He may not understand it yet, but in time, he'll realize how much we've done for him."

They clinked glasses, celebrating their so-called "achievement" as the young tribesman lay sleeping, far from the home he longed for, lost in a world he couldn't understand. In their ambition, Aryan and Tina failed to see the hollowness of their actions, blind to the suffering they had inflicted in the name of progress.

They believed they were bringing enlightenment, but in reality, they had stripped away his peace, forcing him into a life of fear and alienation. And as the night wore on, the quiet of the room only deepened the emptiness of their so-called success, a reminder of how far they had drifted from the humanity they claimed to serve.

CHAPTER THIRTEEN

The Price of Progress

Days passed, and Aryan and Tina continued with their project, oblivious to the toll it was taking on the young tribesman. They were busy with their plans and too preoccupied to notice the quiet suffering of their guest, who had grown weaker and more withdrawn with each new exposure to the modern world. Then, one morning, they found him lying in bed, his body flushed with fever, his skin covered in red, itchy rashes.

Alarmed, Aryan and Tina immediately called for a doctor. But each doctor they contacted turned down their request, unwilling to treat a patient whose physiology and immunity were so unfamiliar. One doctor even admitted, "We don't know anything about his health history. Treating him would be like experimenting on a stranger."

As the hours passed, the tribesman's condition worsened. He grew delirious with fever, his body trembling, and his breathing grew shallow. The situation spiraled into a crisis as Aryan and Tina were flooded with angry calls from their company, demanding they "fix" the situation immediately. The media had begun to catch wind of the project, and negative attention was building up, putting pressure on the company to resolve it quickly.

In desperation, they finally found an old doctor, a man in his eighties with a reputation for unconventional treatments and herbal remedies. He arrived at their apartment with a small bag of hand-crushed herbs and vegetables, carrying an air of experience and wisdom.

The doctor took one look at the young tribesman, his face hardening as he examined him. "You've put this boy through a terrible ordeal," he muttered as he ground leaves and vegetables into a thick paste, blending it with water to create a natural juice. "All this for what? Your ambition?"

Aryan felt a twinge of discomfort at the doctor's words, but he kept silent. Tina, on the other hand, rolled her eyes slightly, impatient for a solution.

The doctor approached the young man gently, helping him to sit up and sip the greenish juice. The tribesman swallowed a little, coughing weakly, but some color returned to his face as the juice began to take effect. The doctor's touch was tender, almost fatherly, and the tribesman's tense expression softened, as if sensing the care in the old man's hands.

When he finished, the doctor turned to Aryan and Tina, his eyes cold and disapproving. "This boy is suffering, not just from the fever but from everything you've put him through. His body wasn't made to endure the chaos and pollution of this world. What were you thinking, bringing him here against his will?"

Aryan felt his heart sink, memories flooding back of Rishi's words, the warnings he had ignored. The doctor's scolding voice echoed what Rishi had once said, words Aryan had dismissed in his blind pursuit of success.

"Do you even understand what you've done to him?" the doctor continued. "You took him from his home, away from the life he knew, and threw him into a world that means nothing to him. He's a human being, not a test subject."

Tina, eager to end the conversation, reached into her purse and pulled out some money, extending it to the doctor with a forced smile. "Thank you for your help, doctor. Here, please take this."

The doctor looked at the money with disdain, waving it away. "I didn't come here for your money," he replied sharply. "I came here because this boy needed help. But don't mistake my kindness for support of what you're doing. This project of yours—it's cruelty disguised as progress."

With those words, the doctor left, leaving Aryan and Tina in uncomfortable silence.

The media soon caught wind of the tribesman's worsening condition, and the backlash was swift and intense. Headlines condemned the project as unethical, invasive, and harmful, putting immense pressure on the company. Within hours, Aryan and Tina were summoned to the company headquarters, where their supervisor berated them for their carelessness.

"You have one week to fix this," he said coldly, pointing at both of them. "Make this mess go away, or your careers will suffer for it."

Back in their apartment, Aryan and Tina discussed their options. They decided that the only solution was to return the young man to his island as quickly as possible, hoping to avoid further damage to their reputations. It was a risky decision, but they felt they had no other choice.

Early the next morning, Aryan and Tina packed their things, ready to take the young tribesman back to his home.

But just as they were about to leave, they noticed that he was lying very still, his breaths shallow and labored. Aryan approached him, checking his pulse, and felt his heart sink as he realized the young man had passed away during the night.

Tina sighed in frustration, her mind immediately turning to the implications. "This complicates everything," she said. "Let's bury him here, somewhere discreet, and tell the company we returned him to the island. No one has to know."

Aryan was taken aback, a surge of guilt and sorrow filling him. "No, Tina. We can't do that. He deserves to be laid to rest on his homeland. We owe him that much."

Tina's eyes narrowed, her voice cold and dismissive. "Aryan, be realistic. No one will know. Just bury him here, and let's be done with this. We can move on and forget about it."

But Aryan couldn't bring himself to agree. Rishi's words echoed in his mind, the warnings about his blind ambition, the sacrifices he had made in the name of success. In that moment, he realized how far he had strayed from the values he once held dear, the humanity he had abandoned along the way.

"I can't do this anymore, Tina," Aryan said firmly, his voice filled with a sadness he couldn't hide. "I'm taking him back to the island."

They argued, but Aryan was resolute. Finally, Tina relented, though she was visibly angry, refusing to go along with his decision. She left, leaving Aryan alone to fulfill the promise he felt he owed.

That evening, Aryan placed the young man's body on a small boat, gently wrapping him in a cloth as a sign of respect. As he sailed away from the city, his heart was heavy with regret and shame, each wave against the boat's hull reminding him of the choices that had led him here.

The voyage was quiet, and with only the sea around him, Aryan found himself alone with his thoughts. Memories flooded his mind—of his family, of Rishi, of the life he had once known before ambition consumed him. He thought about Rishi's sacrifices, the faith his friend had placed in him, only to be betrayed by Aryan's own selfish choices.

As he neared the island, he looked down at the still figure of the tribesman, a painful reminder of his failure. He had chased success, believing it would bring him happiness and fulfillment, only to realize that he had lost himself in the process. The people who had once mattered, the values he had once cherished—all of it had been abandoned in the name of progress.

In the stillness of the night, with only the stars as witnesses, Aryan felt a tear slip down his cheek, the weight of his actions settling over him like a heavy shroud. He had taken a life, a culture, and twisted it for his own gain, only to realize that in the end, he had gained nothing.

As he approached the island, he felt a deep, unshakeable sorrow—a sense that he could never undo the harm he had caused. He anchored the boat near the shore, carrying the young tribesman's body gently onto the sand. He laid him down with reverence, saying a quiet prayer in his own language, hoping that somehow, the young man's spirit would find peace.

CHAPTER FOURTEEN

A Different Kind of Wisdom

As Aryan stood by the shore, the young tribesman's body resting gently on the sand, he felt a growing fear gnawing at him. He hadn't planned on being seen by the tribe, but as dawn broke, he noticed figures emerging from the trees. One by one, the tribespeople appeared, surrounding him and the body of their young kin.

Aryan's heart pounded in his chest, expecting anger, perhaps even violence. He had taken one of their own, and now he had returned him lifeless. But as he watched, something completely unexpected happened.

Instead of displaying sadness or outrage, the tribespeople began to dance. Their faces held no sorrow—only joy, as they raised their hands to the sky and moved to a rhythm Aryan couldn't hear. They shouted and sang, their voices rising in unison, celebrating as though this was a moment of great honor.

Aryan watched, stunned, as they lifted the young man's body, carrying him toward the water's edge. They didn't mourn; instead, they danced and shouted, their expressions filled with reverence. Aryan felt his fear dissipate, replaced by confusion and awe as he watched them perform what looked like a sacred ritual.

The tribespeople continued their dance, escorting the body into the shallow waters of the shore. Once there, they gently laid him down, letting the waves lap over him as if offering him to the ocean. They stepped back, still singing, their voices rising to the sky as the sea carried the young man away. Aryan stood in silence, unable to comprehend the depth of their customs, the strange beauty of their farewell.

That night, the tribe welcomed Aryan to stay, and he found himself lying awake, staring at the star-filled sky. His mind reeled from what he had witnessed. He felt a strange sense of calm, as if he had been invited to share in something profound that he didn't yet understand.

Just then, he noticed one of the tribesmen carving into the mountain face nearby, his hands working slowly and deliberately. Intrigued, Aryan approached, his footsteps careful, and watched as the tribesman etched symbols and shapes into the rock. Each stroke seemed purposeful, filled with meaning.

Aryan observed closely, piecing together the significance of what he saw. Over time, as he continued watching and asking questions through gestures, he began to understand the tribe's perspective on life, death, and the world around them.

<u>A New Understanding</u>

Birth and Death as Gifts: Aryan realized that for the tribe, life and death were seen as sacred gifts from their god, the Sun. Birth was celebrated with joy, and death was honored in the same way, as a return to the divine. They believed each phase was part of a grand cycle, worthy of reverence.

Celebration of Life and Death: Both birth and death were celebrated in the same joyful manner. They believed that mourning was unnecessary, for each soul was meant to return to the Sun, completing its journey. Their dances and chants weren't expressions of sorrow but of gratitude for the time given.

The Island as the World, the Ocean as the Gateway to God: For the tribe, the island was their entire world, and the ocean marked the boundary to the divine. They believed the Sun traveled across the sky each day, sinking into the ocean at night. The sea, to them, was a sacred pathway to god, where the souls of their loved ones would journey to reunite with the Sun.

The Ritual of Returning the Dead to the Ocean: The tribe left their dead in the ocean, believing it was the soul's way of reaching the Sun. By letting the body drift away, they were sending the soul on a journey home, where it would be welcomed by their god.

Seeing Aryan, Tina, and the Boatman as Angels: Aryan was stunned to learn that the tribe had viewed him, Tina, and the boatman as messengers from the Sun when they had first arrived. To them, anyone coming from the ocean was sent by their god. They had assumed the Sun had a purpose for their young kin and had taken him for some grand reason, as a test or a sacred journey.

Carving the Purpose Completed: The tribesman carving into the rock was recording what he believed was the fulfillment of a divine purpose. The young man had returned, albeit lifeless, and to the tribe, this meant his journey had ended. He had served his purpose and was called back by the Sun, his spirit now part of something greater.

As Aryan absorbed these insights, a wave of emotion swept over him. He was overwhelmed by the tribe's kindness, their deep connection to nature, and their wisdom, which far exceeded anything he had found in his own world of ambition. In his relentless pursuit of success, he had overlooked the simple yet profound understanding that this tribe had cultivated over generations.

He broke down, tears streaming down his face as he finally grasped the depth of their way of life—a life rich with meaning, free from the rat race, ego, and cruelty that defined his world. Here, people lived with humility, a bond with nature, and a belief in something greater than themselves. They had food, shelter, and most importantly, freedom—the freedom to live and die in harmony with the world around them.

Memories of his old friend, Rishi, filled his mind. He missed Rishi desperately, longing to speak with him, to share the revelations he had uncovered. Rishi's words echoed in his heart, each reminder of kindness and humility a painful reminder of the choices Aryan had made. He realized how much he had lost, how deeply he had strayed from the values they once shared.

The following morning, with a heart full of sorrow and newfound respect, Aryan bid farewell to the tribe. He boarded the small boat, setting sail back to Berlin, leaving the island behind but carrying with him a profound sense of understanding.

As he watched the island fade into the distance, Aryan felt a bittersweet ache in his chest. He knew he could never fully return to the life he had known, for the wisdom of the tribe had forever changed him. They had shown him the truth of life, a truth he had been too blind to see in his quest for success.

And as the waves carried him back to Berlin, Aryan resolved to seek out his friend, hoping that somehow, he could rebuild what he had lost, and live a life filled not with ambition, but with purpose, humility, and love.

CHAPTER FIFTEEN

THE FALL

Aryan returned to Berlin a changed man, carrying the lessons he had learned from the tribe like a weight on his heart. The profound realization of how far he had drifted from humanity and kindness had left him raw, vulnerable, and longing for connection. But upon arriving at the office, he was met with cold news. He and Tina had been terminated from their positions due to the negative media attention and the failure of their project.

The news struck him hard. For the first time, he felt the deep sting of regret—not because he had lost his position, but because he had poured everything into a path that ultimately left him empty and alone. The once-coveted success he had chased now seemed hollow. Aryan retreated into himself, spending the next few days in isolation, haunted by memories of the tribespeople, their joyful simplicity, and his old friend Rishi, who had tried to guide him back to humanity long before.

Aryan's health began to decline. He became feverish and weak, plagued by headaches and chills. Exhausted and lost, he sank into a physical and emotional low. His once-practical, efficient mind now seemed unable to cope with the weight of his memories, regrets, and a strange fungal infection he had contracted on his journey back.

Meanwhile, Tina, ever the pragmatist, had already started looking for new job opportunities. She was focused, determined to find stability, her mind fixated on the future with no room for reflection or emotion. Aryan's illness seemed an inconvenience to her, one she tried to ignore as she went about her search.

But as Aryan's condition worsened, his symptoms became impossible to overlook. His skin bore strange red patches, his body weakened, and his fever worsened. Finally, Tina took him to the hospital, concerned but primarily eager to get him the help he needed so she could resume her search uninterrupted.

The hospital staff, however, took one look at Aryan's worsening fungal infection and turned them away. The doctor explained that his illness was highly contagious and potentially dangerous, and they lacked the specialized facilities to treat him safely. Tina's frustration grew as she struggled to find someone who would help, but each attempt was met with rejection.

Exasperated and angry, Tina finally lost her patience. "I can't keep doing this, Aryan," she said, her voice cold and detached. "I have my own life to worry about. I can't risk everything for you."

She left him alone in their apartment that night, packing her belongings swiftly and leaving without another word. As the door closed behind her, Aryan lay alone, feverish and weak, the realization of his isolation settling over him like a shroud. He was left with only his thoughts and the painful awareness of the choices that had led him to this point.

As Aryan's illness became apparent to his neighbors, they grew concerned for their own safety. Worried about the contagion, they alerted the police and called for an ambulance, hoping to find a way to deal with the situation without endangering themselves. But even the authorities were wary, unwilling to take on a case that could spread an unknown infection.

With no options left, the authorities made a decision. They transported Aryan, barely conscious and too weak to resist, to the harbor. There, they placed him in a small boat, leaving him with a few supplies—water, some food, and a thin blanket. The boat was untied, and as it drifted away from the shore, the sound of the harbor faded, leaving Aryan in haunting silence.

Alone on the boat, Aryan's eyes welled with tears as he realized the full extent of his helplessness. His body trembled, too weak to sit up, and his arms felt like lead. He tried to call out, but his voice was barely a whisper, swallowed by the vastness of the sea. All he could do was lie there, his mind racing with regrets and memories of a life he had forsaken in pursuit of an empty dream.

Weakly, he reached for the water and took a sip, feeling the cool liquid slide down his parched throat. The food lay beside him, untouched, as he couldn't muster the strength to eat. He lay on his back, gazing up at the fading light as the boat drifted along, guided only by the wind and waves.

In his delirium, Aryan's thoughts turned to Rishi. Memories of their friendship, their laughter, and Rishi's gentle guidance played in his mind like a comforting lullaby. In his weakened state, he longed for Rishi's presence, his kindness, and the unwavering support he had taken for granted. The thought of Rishi brought him a fleeting sense of comfort, a faint hope that somehow, if he could only see his friend again, everything might be all right.

As darkness fell, Aryan slipped in and out of consciousness, the boat rocking gently beneath him. The sky above was vast and indifferent, filled with stars that seemed to stretch on forever. Aryan's breathing grew shallow, and he drifted deeper into a half-dream, his mind filled with images of the island, the tribe, and the life he had left behind.

In his mind, he saw Rishi's face, filled with warmth and compassion, as if urging him to hold on, to find his way back to the person he had once been. Aryan's lips moved in a faint whisper, barely audible over the sound of the waves.

"Rishi... I'm so sorry," he murmured, a tear slipping down his cheek.

The boat continued to drift, swallowed by the darkness of the night, carrying Aryan toward an unknown fate. The vast expanse of the sea stretched endlessly around him, the silence broken only by the soft lapping of the waves. Aryan lay motionless, his mind hovering between dreams and reality, lost in a deep, quiet sorrow as the world faded into darkness.

And so, under the stars and guided by nothing but the wind, Aryan's journey continued, drifting ever onward, his fate left to the mercy of the sea.

CHAPTER SIXTEEN

The Return to Simplicity

Aryan lay on the small boat, his body weak, drifting between dreams and reality. His fevered mind took him back through the years, flashing memories of his childhood, his town, and his family. He saw his parents' proud faces, the dusty streets of his hometown, his shelves full of awards, and the countless hours he had spent working on his research, driven by ambition and the pursuit of success.

In his dreams, he could see Rishi, his face filled with kindness, and he felt an ache in his heart as he remembered the friend who had once been by his side. Rishi had believed in him, had given up so much for him, only for Aryan to leave him behind. Lost in these memories, Aryan was barely aware of his surroundings as the boat drifted along, carried by the wind and waves.

Then, suddenly, he felt a familiar touch, warm and gentle, like the memory of his mother's hand from when he was a child. With great difficulty, he opened his eyes, squinting against the brightness. He couldn't believe what he was seeing.

Standing around him were the tribespeople—the very people he had visited on the remote island, the ones he had wronged by taking one of their own. His boat, by some twist of fate, had drifted back to the island. He was filled with wonder and relief as he saw their familiar faces, though he feared they would resent him for his past actions.

But to his surprise, there was no anger in their eyes. They approached him without hesitation, their faces kind and open, showing no fear of his illness or his weakened state. One of the tribesmen, a man with gentle eyes, lifted Aryan from the boat, carrying him as if he were a family member returning home. Another tribeswoman brought over a fresh coconut, cracking it open and offering him the sweet water within.

With great care, they carried him from the shore to their village, laying him down on a soft bed of grass, shaded by the trees. They brought clean water to bathe him, using herbs and leaves from the forest to cleanse his body. One by one, they cared for him, wiping away the sweat from his fevered skin and whispering soft, comforting words in their language, words Aryan didn't understand but felt in his heart.

Days passed, and the tribespeople continued to care for him, offering him food gathered from the forest and water from the lakes. They sang songs around him at night, their voices soothing, filling the quiet night air with a warmth he hadn't felt in years. Aryan felt a sense of peace and healing, and slowly, his strength began to return. The infection that had once ravaged his body started to subside, the fever broke, and he felt his body growing stronger under the tribe's gentle care.

As the weeks went by, Aryan felt himself adapting to their way of life. He learned to walk through the forest, following the tribesmen as they showed him how to find food—roots, fruits, and edible plants growing abundantly in the wild. When he was thirsty, he would drink from clear, cool lakes, feeling the refreshing purity of the water. For the first time in his life, he experienced a life without competition, without ambition, without the constant chase for more.

He discovered the pleasure of simple tasks, helping the tribe with fishing, gathering fruits, and tending to small fires that provided warmth during the night. With every passing day, Aryan felt a part of the tribe, sharing in their work, laughter, and joy. They showed him how to make tools from wood and stone, how to weave baskets from leaves, and how to appreciate the beauty in the simplest things.

At dawn, he would join them in their ritual of worshipping the Sun, raising his hands to the sky as the golden light touched the island. He understood now the depth of their beliefs—the Sun was life to them, its cycle marking their days and guiding their lives. Aryan found comfort in these rituals, feeling a connection to something larger than himself, something peaceful and enduring.

In the evenings, they would sit together by the fire, sharing stories through gestures and expressions, laughing together over tales Aryan could only half understand. Yet, in those moments, he felt a deep, unspoken bond with each of them. They accepted him as one of their own, without questions, without judgment, giving him a place among them as naturally as the trees belonged to the forest.

The days rolled by in gentle succession, each one filled with a quiet purpose. Aryan had no need for the rat race he had once lived for, no need for recognition or success. If he wanted food, he gathered it himself. If he was thirsty, he would drink from a stream or a coconut. If he needed rest, he lay on the soft grass, listening to the sounds of the forest, the rustling leaves, the distant calls of birds. He was at peace in a way he had never known before.

In this life, he found a happiness he had long forgotten. There was no competition, no rush, no greed—only a quiet contentment, a belonging he hadn't felt since childhood. For the first time, he felt truly free.

As he lay one evening under the starlit sky, watching the stars twinkle above, Aryan's thoughts drifted to his old life, the life he had left behind. He thought of his parents, his sister, and, above all, Rishi. He wished he could tell Rishi about this life, about the peace he had found here. He missed his friend, missed the love and support Rishi had given him without asking for anything in return.

Now, Aryan understood what Rishi had tried to teach him—that life was about more than success and recognition, that real happiness lay in the bonds we shared, in kindness and simplicity. Aryan felt a tear slip down his cheek, not of sadness, but of gratitude for the journey that had led him here.

The tribespeople continued to care for him, celebrating his recovery as they celebrated all of life—with joy, laughter, and the belief that every moment was a gift. And as Aryan looked around at his new family, he knew he had finally found what he had been searching for all along—a life of purpose, a life filled with love, and a life truly worth living.

CHAPTER SEVENTEEN

The Circle Completed

One clear morning, Aryan was walking along the shore, enjoying the cool breeze and the gentle sound of waves lapping against the sand. His life among the tribes had become one of peace and simplicity, but even in this new world, he carried quiet memories of his past. Yet today, something unexpected caught his eye.

In the sand, there were faint marks—letters written in English. Aryan's heart skipped a beat as he crouched down, tracing the letters with his fingers, his mind racing. He couldn't make sense of what he was seeing. Who could have written this? The tribespeople had no knowledge of English.

He ran back to the village and found one of the tribesmen, gesturing and pointing towards the letters on the sand. He tried to ask, hoping they might understand his question. After a few moments, the tribesman seemed to grasp what Aryan was asking and nodded, motioning towards a distant part of the island.

From his gestures, Aryan understood that another tribe, one he had never met, lived near the edge of the island

and sometimes visited his new village. His heart pounded with a mix of curiosity and hope, and he asked eagerly if they could take him to this other village. The tribesman smiled, understanding Aryan's excitement, and called for a few more people to join them on the journey.

Together, Aryan and his guides set off, walking along narrow forest paths shaded by tall trees. Birds chirped above, and the air was filled with the sweet scent of wildflowers. Aryan's mind raced with thoughts, wondering if this other tribe could possibly hold a connection to his past.

They walked for hours, crossing rivers on foot and climbing rocky paths. Aryan felt his anticipation building with each step, the possibility of something wonderful and unexpected just within reach.

Finally, they arrived at the village, nestled in a quiet clearing, surrounded by dense jungle. And there, in the center of the village, Aryan's heart nearly stopped at the sight that awaited him.

In front of him, dressed in tribal attire, was Rishi. His friend, the very person he had thought he would never see again, stood laughing and playing with the children of the village, his face radiating joy and peace. Aryan's heart swelled with emotion as he watched Rishi, who seemed completely at ease, as if he had belonged here all along.

Unable to hold back, Aryan walked forward, his steps slow and steady, wanting to soak in every second of this unbelievable moment. Rishi turned, sensing someone's presence, and his face lit up with shock and joy. Without a word, he ran to Aryan, his eyes filled with tears, and pulled him into a tight embrace. They held each other, overcome with emotions that needed no words, their bond stronger than ever, forged by distance, time, and experiences that only they could understand.

The tribespeople, who lived with such pure hearts, gathered around them, smiling and clapping. To them, this reunion was a beautiful moment, something to celebrate. They didn't question where Aryan or Rishi had come from, or why they had once left. They only saw the happiness in their faces, and that was all that mattered.

As the sun began to set, Aryan and Rishi sat together, surrounded by the warmth of the tribe, sharing stories of their separate journeys, of the paths that had led them back to each other. Aryan told Rishi about his journey into ambition, the lessons he had learned, and the kindness of the tribespeople who had taken him in without question. Rishi shared his story of how, after leaving their town, he had stumbled upon this very island and decided to stay, finding the life he had always dreamed of, free from expectations and full of peace.

As night fell, they made a decision. They would stay here, on this island, among the tribespeople who had shown them a new way of living, a life of freedom, simplicity, and joy. They knew they couldn't return to the world they had once belonged to, a world filled with competition and emptiness. Here, they had found something far more precious—a community that valued life, celebrated each moment, and lived in harmony with the world around them.

In the days that followed, Aryan and Rishi settled into their new lives together, blending with the tribe, sharing in their work, their laughter, and their rituals. They became part of the community, their presence welcomed by the people who lived without fear or cruelty, sharing everything they had, including happiness.

And so, their lives continued on the island, where the ocean met the sky, where the sun rose and set with the rhythm of life itself. Here, they had found what they had both been searching for—a life filled with peace, friendship, and the simplicity of truly living.

The story of Aryan and Rishi ended not with a return to the life they had left behind, but with a new beginning, where they could finally be free to live as they had always wanted, hand in hand with nature, their hearts open and their spirits at rest.

Thank You

Thank You to My Readers

Dear Readers,

Thank you for joining Aryan and Rishi's journey in *The Lost Path to Home.* I hope their story touched your hearts and offered reflections on the importance of kindness, connection, and simplicity in our fast-paced world. Writing this book has been a deeply meaningful experience, and I am grateful to each of you for taking the time to explore its pages and its message. Your support and interest mean so much, as stories come to life only when shared.

As this journey concludes, know that there are more stories in the works, each with new characters, places, and themes that I hope will intrigue, inspire, and connect us even more. I look forward to sharing these with you soon. Until then, may we all find joy in the simple, meaningful moments in our own lives.

With heartfelt thanks,

Why Aryan & Rishi ?

The names Aryan and Rishi hold special significance. Aryan represents ambition and strength, qualities that drive him toward success but can also lead him astray. Rishi, on the other hand, embodies wisdom and peace, guiding Aryan back to what is essential. Their names mirror the qualities they represent, creating a balance that is central to the story's message.

My Journey With The Banking On Love Series

Dear Readers,

Thank you for exploring *The Lost Path to Home.* I'm thrilled to share that I have also published two previous books—*Banking on Love: A Tale of Hearts & Balance Sheets* and *Banking on Love 2: A Tale of Determination.* These stories blend life, relationships, and resilience, set against the backdrop of the banking world. Currently, I'm working on the third installment, *Banking on Love 3: A Tale of Perhaps & Misunderstandings,* which promises to explore the complexities of relationships with fresh twists.

These books are available on Amazon, Flipkart, and the Notion Press website. Your encouragement and feedback mean a lot to me. Thank you for reading and supporting my journey!

www.ingramcontent.com/pod-product-compliance
Lightning Source LLC
LaVergne TN
LVHW021159160826
845679LV00024B/2172

* 9 7 9 8 8 9 6 1 0 4 3 5 3 *